BUGS

BUGS

Sarah Creese

make
believe
ideas

Beastly bugs can have many eyes!
They are bright and colorful
and masters of disguise.
With a stinger, or pincers, wings or a shell;
all bugs are different and amazing as well!

Reading together

This book is an ideal first reader for your child, combining simple words and sentences with stunning color photography of real-life bugs.
Here are some of the many ways you can help your child take those first steps in reading.
Encourage your child to:

- Look at and explore the detail in the pictures.

- Sound out the letters in each word.

- Read and repeat each short sentence.

Look at the pictures

Make the most of each page by talking about the pictures and finding key words. Here are some questions you can use to discuss each page as you go along:

- Why do you like this bug?

- What would it feel like to touch?

- What color is it?

- What is special about this bug?

Look at rhymes

Some of the sentences in this book are simple rhymes. Encourage your child to recognize rhyming words. Try asking the following questions:

- What does this word say?

- Can you find a word that rhymes with it?

- Look at the ending of two words that rhyme. Are they spelled the same? For example, "lunch" and "crunch," and "prey" and "day."

Test understanding

It is one thing to understand the meaning of individual words, but you need to make sure that your child understands the facts in the text.

- Play "find the obvious mistake." Read the text as your child looks at the words with you, but make an obvious mistake to see if he or she catches it. Ask your child to correct you and provide the right word.

- After reading the facts, close the book and think up questions to ask your child.

- Make statements about the bugs and ask your child whether the statements are true or false.

- Provide your child with three answers to a question and ask him or her to pick the correct one.

Quiz pages

At the end of the book there is a simple quiz. Ask the questions and see if your child can remember the right answers from the text. If not, encourage him or her to look up the answers.

Bugs

Bugs come in all shapes and sizes and can be found all over the world.

Demoiselle Damselfly

They can have hundreds
of legs, amazing patterns,
wonderful wings, or fierce
pincers and stingers!

I am a spider,
with eight thin legs.
I catch my dinner
in a silky web.

Wasp Spider

I have two pairs
of buzzing wings.
I make honey, but watch
out for my sting!

Honeybee

I use strong pincers
to hold my prey.
I hunt at night
and hide during the day.

Emperor Scorpion

stinger

pincer

legs

mouth

13

I'm a hungry caterpillar,
I munch and crunch.
A tasty dish of leaves
is my favorite lunch.

body

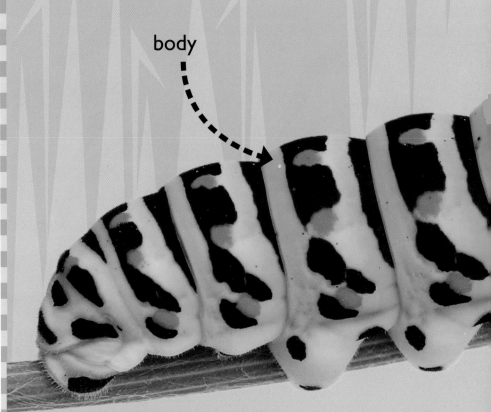

Swallowtail Caterpillar

Caterpillars feeding

false leg

leg

I'm a colorful butterfly.
My favorite thing to eat
is nectar from a flower—
it is sticky and sweet!

**Red-Haired Day
Butterfly**

Swallowtail Butterfly

Monarch Butterfly

Tiger Butterfly

Red Admiral Butterfly

I'm a leaf-cutter ant—
with no time to rest!
I collect leaves
to take back
to my nest.

Leaf-Cutter Ant

Army Ant

Black Ant

Weaver Ant

Trap-Jaw Ant

I keep hidden,
and then I strike!
I hold my prey
with legs covered in spikes.

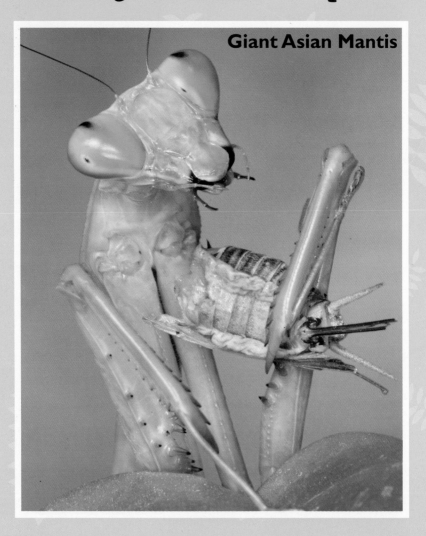

Giant Asian Mantis

head

spike

Spiny Flower Mantis

wings

Rhinoceros Beetle

Tiger Beetle

Dung Beetle

Cardinal Beetle

Ladybug

I am a ladybug,
watch me fly!
I'm red and black
and I zoom around the sky!

Dragonfly

I'm a dragonfly.
I'm a beautiful sight!

Red Percher Dragonfly

I can hover in the air.
I am colorful and bright.

My bold, bright stripes
make a colorful display
and help to scare
my enemies away!

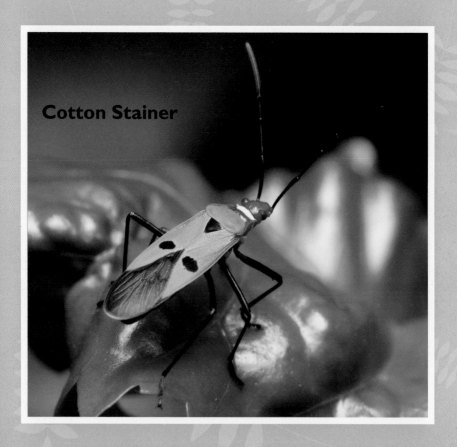

Cotton Stainer

Fire Bug

What do

1. What do butterflies like to eat?

They like to eat nectar from flowers.

2. Which bugs make honey?

Bees make honey.

3. Which bug uses pincers to hold its prey?

Scorpions use pincers to hold their prey.

you know?

4. Which bugs catch their dinner in a web?

Spiders catch their dinner in a web.

5. What do caterpillars like to eat?

Caterpillars like to eat leaves.

6. Which bug takes leaves back to its nest?

The leaf-cutter ant takes leaves back to its nest.

Useful words

hungry
When you are hungry, you need to eat food.

honey
Honey is sticky and sweet.
Bees make honey.

web
Spiders make webs to catch bugs.
They make it using their silk.

nectar
Flowers make nectar.
Bugs like to eat it because it is sweet.

nest
A nest is a safe home for animals and their young.

Key words

Here are some key words used in context.
Make simple sentences for the other words
in the border.

I hide in the **day**.

I make honey.

I am **a** bug.

I hover **in** the air.

Watch me fly **away**!

BUGS

Ready to Read combines simple words and sentences with amazing photographs to provide inspiring first reading books that children will love to read together, read with help—and read alone!

PRE-LEVEL 1
- FIRST WORDS
- WORD REPETITION
- ABC'S

LEVEL 1
- BEGINNING TO READ
- SIMPLE SENTENCES
- SIGHT WORDS

LEVEL 2
- READING ALONE
- LONGER SENTENCES
- FACT BOXES

LEVEL 3
- READING PROFICIENTLY
- RICHER VOCABULARY
- PARAGRAPHS AND SHORT CHAPTERS

$4.99 U.S. $5.99 Canada

ISBN10: 1-84879-684-6
ISBN13: 978-1-84879-684-3

5 0 4 9 9

9 781848 796843

04201102

Printed and bound in Dongguan, China, April 2011.
Conforms to safety requirements of CPSIA and ASTM